Call Me
Quixote

Call Me Quixote

GENTA SEBASTIAN

ISBN: 978-1-942594-17-8

Dedication

For Mabel Teng
2004 San Francisco Assessor-Recorder

~*~*~

We were your Dulcinea.
You saw the oppressed and despised
as precious and rare,
and treated those gathered with a respect and dignity
we didn't expect,
unprepared for consideration or kindness.
I've wondered about something for twenty years.
You sent the port-a-potties,
Didn't you?

CONTENTS

Introduction

During the long Valentine's/President's Day weekend in 2004, Gavin Newsom, then mayor of San Francisco, authorized the release of legal marriage certificates to same-sex couples for the first time in the United States. A thousand weddings were performed by volunteers in City Hall. It was a bold move in the intricate legal game of Gay Rights, as we called them then.

Mayor Newsom's liberal two steps forward would be pushed back by homophobic legislation limiting the civil rights of five to ten percent of the human population. Every couple taking part in the historic events of that weekend knew we probably wouldn't be allowed to stay married...but hope springs eternal.

How did I, a middle-aged woman in comfortable shoes, end up taking a stand for marital rights in a place over two thousand miles from home? Why take the chance? What did I get out of it?

This is the story of putting my love on the line.

Call Me Quixote

Chris, the official Best Friend, built a campfire up as wedding guests lingered in the early autumn afternoon. "Hey, who caught Tara's bouquet before she and Myke took off for their honeymoon?"

"I did." Georgia, a long-legged redhead threw the pretty flowers across the campfire at Chris. "And now you have."

"Not me." The tired young woman in her tuxedo pants and unbuttoned vest laughed as she caught them. "Oh no, I helped plan the wedding and stood up for Myke as her Best Friend, and that's all. I'm not the marrying type." She dangled the bouquet over the campfire.

"Oh no you don't. Pass them over here." Her girlfriend, Jen, snickered as she snatched them from her butch's fingers. "*I'm* the marrying kind."

"Ooooh." The dispersing group of friends laughed comfortably, knowingly. Chris might protest, but she and Jen were a long-time couple; they might not be married, but as close as you can get without paperwork.

Handing the bouquet back to Georgia, she shrugged. "Here you go, you caught these fair and square.

Sleep with one of the flowers under your pillow and you'll see the face of your true love in your dreams."

"Yeah, Jen doesn't need them." Chris rolled her dress shirt to the elbows, winking at her girlfriend. "All she's got to do is roll over and open her eyes."

Joking, hugging, promising to get together soon, wedding guests waved happily from their cars, leaving the rented campsite to the newlyweds' best friends to clean up. The three pitched a tent earlier and would spend the night.

The last person remaining, the wedding officiant, joined the small group at the fire. The elder handed the signed marriage certificate to Chris. "I understand you're in charge of this?" She glanced around at the younger faces looking back at her. "My ride called. She's got a flat tire and it'll be after dark before she picks me up." She held up a flask of whiskey. "May I join you while I wait?"

"Of course." Jen took the pretty vellum paper to examine. She pulled a paperclipped business card free. "Your name is Quixote?" She pronounced it 'Ki-shoat'.

Chris took back the certificate to see for herself. "I read it 'Kee-hoe-tay'." She examined the business card attached. "Dawn Quixote." She grinned across the fire at the older woman standing beside the log where Georgia sat. "Like the knight errant, Cervantes' Quixote?" She searched the round woman's wrinkled face for signs of a joke, then shook her head. "He was a crazy, sad-faced fictional character. No one's named after *him*." Jen elbowed her in the side.

"Well, you're partially right, Quixote is a fictional

character, and it's my DBA, Doing Business As name." Bright eyes and a wide smile charmed them completely. "Not the name I was born with, granted, but it's a legal one."

"Sorry, I didn't mean to be rude," Chris grinned, "but you certainly don't have a woeful countenance." She gestured to an open log at the fire. "You look like a very pleasant person who shares whiskey at campfires, not a madman given to tilting at windmills or worshipping a poor prostitute, so forgive me. Please, Quixote, join us while you wait."

"You can call me Q." As she laughed, her generous, matronly bosom jiggled under a full-length robe of deep purple. "Quixote is the name I use as an officiant." She pointed at the marriage certificate.

"If you don't mind my asking, why choose Quixote?" Georgia scooted over to make room on the log beside her.

"Why?" Q handed her the whiskey flask before removing and folding her robe. She looked much more relaxed in a full-length swirling tunic of heavy linen. Embroidered with designs in fabulous colors, it glittered in the flickering firelight as she seated herself on the log beside Georgia. "That's my name for love." She laughed. "And, I have a healthy fear of needles."

The three younger women took a moment to absorb her words. They raised their eyebrows at each other as they drank Quixote's whiskey, their curiosity piqued.

"There *must* be a story to explain that." Jen

giggled, passing back her flask. She laughed delightedly when Q winked at her with a nod.

"I'd love to hear it." Georgia sighed. "The wedding put me in the mood for a good love story."

Chris smiled gently at their single friend. "You're always in the mood for a good love story."

"This campfire and friendly gathering put me in the mood for s'mores." The plump old lady nodded at a paper bag holding graham crackers, a bag of marshmallows, and bundle of chocolate bars. "I haven't had one in years. Tell you what, I'll trade you my story for a s'more."

"Done." Chris jumped up from her log. "Let us pick up from the wedding while we can still see and find some sticks for roasting. And after, my woman has a couple of blunts ready to share."

The three got busy taking turns ducking into their tent to reemerge in jeans or sweats. Each with their own bag for trash, it took less time to dispose of ribbons, garlands, and the few leftover plastic cups and paper plates, than to tell it.

Georgia built up the fire and by the time the sun set, each of the four watched their browning marshmallow puff over the fire. They smoked Jen's weed and slathered chocolate layered graham crackers with the hot, gooey treats. To wash down the s'mores, Chris popped the cork of a bottle of sparkling wine and filled four plastic champagne flutes.

"To Myke and Tara." Q raised hers. "May they live together in peace and harmony, increasing their joy every day." Sticky lips and tongues repeated Q's toast around the fire.

"I wonder where they are?" Jen gazed into the flames.

Chris looked at the watch on her wrist. "They should be pulling in to airport parking about now. Their plane leaves for Paris in three hours."

"What a wonderful choice for a honeymoon." Q unpinned two thick grey braids wrapped around her head and they fell heavily to her waist. "They'll have a romantic, magical time."

She passed the joint, shaking her head. "So many things are legal now that used to get you thrown into jail." She laughed, ironically. "When I was a teen, people were given life sentences for having a single seed in their possession. Seems impossible now, but it happened."

Q sighed, sipped her wine, and cleared her throat. Her voice, aged and mellow, carried clearly. "And now I'll keep my part of the bargain. I promised you the story of how I became a modern-day Quixote. It begins as every good love story does. I met a woman and fell in love."

She winked and smiled at the group. "You know how it is."

They grinned and nodded their heads. Yes, they knew.

"It wasn't illegal for us to marry in the United States when we met at the turn of the century."

"What do you mean, not illegal?" Jen leaned forward, her shoulder length brown bob framing her round face. "Then what was all the protesting about?"

7

Q snorted. "It wasn't illegal because no one ever thought about it. Bigots had to pass legislation and enact laws to restrict marriage to one man and one woman. It wasn't an issue until bigotry made it controversial. Until then, it was unimaginable."

She smiled around at the young people. "The world tilted catawampus the first time I heard the phrase *gay marriage.* What were those two words even doing together?" She shrugged. "Like that could even happen, right? Crazy talk. The concept had *never* occurred to me, quite literally inconceivable. But when my vision of the world righted itself again, the notion *became* imaginable." Her eyes sparkled by firelight.

"The idea spread, and people began taking it seriously. It seemed not only possible but even likely, before the bigots began overreacting, screeching about 'protecting the sanctity of marriage'. And I wanted to marry my lover, to protect her.

"You see, I'd already declared war on my own country."

Chris' chiseled young face gleamed by the light of the flames as she sipped her drink. "Ya gotta love a take charge woman." She smiled indulgently at Jen.

"As luck would have it, my wife does." Q's wide smile brightened the night.

"Why declare war on America?" Jen pulled a pinner and a lighter from her shirt pocket, shaking her head. "Seems kind of futile. Government's so big it's got us wrapped up nice and tight. The two parties are the same, every politician is crooked, and nothing ever changes."

Chris nodded her head, taking the glowing joint from her girlfriend. "She's right. There's not much anyone can do about it." She inhaled deeply and passed it.

Q hit it while considering the younger women. She blew a thick smoke ring over their heads. "Nothing anyone can do? Don't you girls know, insisting on your rights is your obligation, no matter the odds. Doesn't matter, zilch, nada, not one whit, how many times you get knocked down." She shook her head, making her braids shimmy. "It's how many times a person gets back up that shapes your destiny. I picked myself up and became Quixote because there's nothing more important to fight for than love." She held the skinny marijuana cigarette out for Georgia.

"Oh, yes. Story time." Rising, the redhead walked to the other side of the campfire, the better to see Q. She lowered herself to the ground in front of the log where Jen and Chris sat. Stretching her legs toward the heat, she leaned back and finished the nearly spent joint. "I do enjoy a good love story." She flicked the roach in the fire.

Q gazed into the campfire's flames, her eyes watching memories dance among them. "Then, I hope you love mine." Looking across the fire, she focused on her attentive audience and nodded.

Three young women nodded back at the fascinating old lady, already under the spell of her storytelling.

9

~*~

I was already middle-aged when I met Maria Oliveira in the spring of 2000 and, as is tradition with our people, we moved in together shortly afterward. At the age of forty-three I quit gallivanting all over the country, sold my RV, and settled down with a woman of fifty-two in Minnesota of all places. Home is where the heart is and mine chose hers.

My beloved is a soft butch, as defined by herself and her friends as they grew up on a small Portuguese island in the Azores. I am a soft femme, born to comfort and privilege, and although we come from completely different backgrounds and upbringings, we suit one another. Our families accepted our relationship with no trauma. Everyone blended well.

Two years after we moved in together, things took a sharp turn when Maria developed chest pains. Her doctor found major blockages to her heart and three stents were ordered. The first two were placed and she began feeling much better. Due to her sensitivity to the dye, the third was to be scheduled at a future date, but it was moved up abruptly after her sudden run-in with the law.

Butch lesbians and rural law enforcement officers from conservative communities can rub each other the wrong way with just a look. I'm sure the same can be said for all sorts of people, but there's a distinct edginess between cops and masculine presenting females. Maria has a heavy accent and a fiercely independent demeanor that won't be pushed around. One tense night outside a convenience store in rural northern Minnesota, a brief confrontation with a deputy sheriff ended with an abrupt warning for her to get out of town in ten-minutes or be arrested for disturbing his peace.

We were visiting our newborn granddaughter, so Maria drove back to our daughter's house to drop off the eggs and grab me before returning home to the Twin Cities. The third clogged artery responded to her agitation and stress. While explaining why we needed to leave suddenly, her eyes rolled back in her head. She slumped to the floor in front of me.

I was holding the baby, so I shouted at our daughter to get the three nitro pills I'd been given *just in case* from my purse.

In her panic, one went in her mother's left ear. She tried again, and the second went up Maria's nose. The last she finally got under her mother's tongue. By then I'd phoned 911 for an ambulance and handed our daughter her baby.

On my knees beside Maria, her breathing shallow and all color drained from her face, I shouted at her. "Don't you dare die, I just found you." I shook her shoulders, rolling her head between my hands, trying to get a response from her. "I searched for you all my life. I can't lose you now." A very long few minutes passed with me babbling, saying anything to try and bring her back, and our daughter walking in circles around us while anxiously bouncing the agitated infant.

The ambulance arrived just as Maria started

11

coming around. They checked her vitals, asked about symptoms, and I explained about the recent stents. When asked if she wanted to be transported to the hospital my stubborn butch, quite groggy, distrusting of hospitals in general, and deeply embarrassed, croaked out, "No."

"You have to take her," I insisted. "She has a documented medical history; a known blockage. Every minute counts during a heart attack and I hold her medical power of attorney." I used my most authoritative voice. "I'll be responsible. Take her to the hospital.

They turned to her again. "Do *you* want us to take you to the hospital?"

She grimaced, rubbed her chest, and shook her head.

"Sorry, lady. It would be different if she were a man and you two were married. A spouse has legal rights." They began packing up their stuff.

In desperation, I threw a panicked tantrum and Maria relented, letting them take her to the nearest hospital twenty miles away. The driver, a nice young man, gave me directions and told me to park in the Emergency Room lot.

"You'll see the ambulance by the door. I'll take a short cut and we'll already be there when you arrive."

Ten minutes later, after speeding down a long lonely highway, I drove into an empty ER parking lot, the ambulance nowhere in sight. I ran into the waiting room and up to the Admissions window.

"I was told to meet Maria Oliveira here. She might be having a heart attack. The driver said he'd take a shortcut. Are they here?" Clearly upset, my hands shook, and my fingertips turned white as I clutched the barely-there paper-signing shelf.

From behind a thick pane of bullet-proof glass, a bored young hospital worker glanced up from her desk. Wearing tight blue scrubs under a loose red sweater, her feathered bleached curls surrounded a face caked with makeup. A nametag dangling crooked on the sweater read C.C. Crocker, Admissions Clerk.

"The patient's name?"

"Maria Oliveira."

"You'll have to spell it. I can't be expected to know how to spell foreign names." I did and she tapped a few keys, stared at a computer screen I couldn't see, and kept me waiting. "And you are...?"

"Genta Sebastian. I'm her partner, her significant other." That's what we called each other then, a more formal label than merely 'my girlfriend'. "I'm responsible for her."

"But you're not *family*?" One thinly plucked eyebrow rose. "Are you her blood relation, or legally married to one?"

"No, but I hold her medical power of attorney. There's a copy in the car. I'll be right back." She nodded and I went out to the empty lot to get the paper we'd filed for only a few months earlier when her chest pains first started. I held hers, she held mine. We kept copies in several places.

When I fed the POA to the admission clerk through the tiny slot in the glass window she pushed it right back out to me. "I cannot give information concerning a patient in the ER to anyone *except* a member of her immediate family."

"Is Maria even *in* the ER? Where's the ambulance?" I wanted to throttle the brat, but I needed information only she could give me. I reined in my tongue, then bit it when she shook her head at me. She smiled, her crooked stained teeth exposed behind glistening chapped lips. She opened a filing cabinet and gave me the cold shoulder, ignoring my every question.

The wail of an approaching siren sounded, followed by flashing lights. C.C. Crocker disappeared into the back as I raced outside and watched a gurney with Maria lying on it being wheeled through a pair of sliding glass doors. I raced back into the waiting room just as the admissions czar reentered her glass palace.

"That's her, Maria Oliveira. I want to see her." I shook my POA at the glass. "I have a right to see her."

"No. No, you don't. This hospital has a policy that only members of the immediate family can be admitted into the ER to see patients." She grinned nastily. "You're not family. You're nothing."

I have never wanted to hit anyone more.

Just then our daughter rushed through the door, baby granddaughter heavily swaddled in a carrier over her arm. Behind her the red and blue revolving lights of the local sheriff's car now joined the ambulance's white and yellow ones, lighting up the parking lot like a disco dance floor. She hurried over and gave me a hug.

"What's going on?" we both said to each other.

"He showed up at my place to make sure he'd chased Ma out of town. I made him bring us to the hospital to see for himself what he did."

I nodded, unsurprised at the small minded thinking. "She," I tossed my head at eavesdropping Crocker, "says I can't go in to see your mom because I'm not family."

My daughter handed me the baby. She marched up to the glass window and started explaining to the heartless wretch that I was family in every way that mattered and that her mother would definitely want to see me as soon as possible. Her voice grew stronger and more berating as the clerk's refusals became shorter and ruder.

The deputy sheriff strolled through the sliding doors with his thumbs tucked into his belt and the tension in the room ramped up even higher. "How's it going, Cruella?" Probably not her real name but that's how I heard it. His puffy eyes squinted at the glass enclosed local. "You called about some trouble?"

"I've told this woman," she gestured at me, "she can't go in to see her significant other *girlfriend*, if you know what I mean." Her disgusted tone dripped with self-righteousness. "It's hospital policy that only *family* can visit in the ER and now she's harassing me and they're both making a scene."

That was it, the straw that broke this camel's back. "*I* am harassing *you*?" I advanced on C.C. Crocker, glass be damned. "*We* are causing this scene?"

She sneered in my face and the sheriff moved to

15

block me.

"Yeah." He nodded. "Makes sense. I ran a dyke, musta been her lover, outta town a while ago." He laughed. "Or scared her into a heart attack, I guess."

I scanned his smug face, memorizing it. "You did this." I knew it wasn't true, but *damn*, it felt true.

The smug smile on his face started fading as he stared into my eyes.

"Genta! Genta!" I knew my beloved instantly by her low-pitched voice and distinctive Portuguese accent. That, and the fact she kept shouting my name loudly. "Genta? Where are my people? Genta!"

A nurse pushed open the heavy locked door to the ER, peering into the waiting room. "Who's Genta?"

"I am." I handed my sleeping granddaughter to her mother.

"The doctor said to find you." She waved me in. "The patient's growing more and more agitated. We need her to calm down for the test."

Without wasting another moment on either the bully deputy or admissions czar, I followed the nurse back to their noisiest and, at least momentarily, only patient. Maria calmed down at once, greatly relieved when she saw my familiar face among all the strangers. The nurse told me why the ambulance arrived late while I clutched the rails of her gurney.

"Bob, our best EMT, couldn't start an IV on the bumpy back roads. He was struggling to hit a vein, so they pulled over to the side of the road until he could." The middle-aged angel blinked at me through round glasses.

"They also gave Maria more nitro during transport, so you were right to insist."

Soon, Nurse Angel hooked Maria up to a machine that started humming; a pen twitched back and forth across paper. When no one was looking, I reached over the gurney rail, grabbed her hand, and squeezed.

An hour later, with an EKG in hand and the doctor's reassurance she'd suffered serious angina but *not* a heart attack, we hurried home to make an appointment with her surgeon for the third stent as soon as possible.

Once I knew my beloved would survive, a deep anger grew in my heart toward my own country. During one of the worst moments of my life, as I stood before C.C. Crocker terrified and helpless, she took cruel delight in adding to my torture. I have no doubt she would have escalated the situation with the deputy if the doctor and nurse, who outranked her, hadn't called for me. She was free to do so legally because the laws and ordinances of that rural area gave her religion precedence over our relationship, our family, our very lives. That was only one law, among many, that needed to change.

The admissions czar and get-outta-my-town-deputy ignited a flame in my belly with their state-approved bullying. That day I declared war on my own country until they recognize our equality. Enough. Nothing less would do, will do. I am a proud American, a responsible citizen, and I began exercising my right to protest injustice."

~*~

Q fell silent, finishing the champagne in her plastic flute.

"That totally sucked." Chris handed the bottle to Georgia to pass. "What a couple of pussy bitches."

The tall, flannel wearing redhead handed it over to the thirsty storyteller. "Hey, I like pussies and love a couple of bitches." She looked up over her shoulder, laughing disarmingly at her friends to remove any sting from her words. "But those two were horrible so let's call 'em what they are, human garbage."

"Yeah." Jen took her girlfriend's hand, dark eyes troubled. "I'm telling you, if Chris were in the hospital having a medical emergency and they wouldn't let me see her..." She frowned, a sharp V formed between her eyebrows as she scowled. "Well, it wouldn't be pretty."

The old woman filling her glass with sparkling wine chuckled in appreciation of the young femme's ferocity. "Let's just say it's a good thing there was a thick pane of glass between C.C. Crocker and me when she told me I didn't count, or I would have been in jail for putting her in the cemetery." She took a sip, raised her plastic champagne flute to the young women assembled, and said, "But I digress."

~*~

I remember the exact instant I heard the phrase 'gay marriage' for the first time. It was the last weekend in

June 2002, and I was registering voters for a mid-term election at Twin Cities Pride. It was a good crowd that year, full of high spirits. As I cajoled passersby to sign up, a couple of young women walking arm in arm waved me off saying they were already registered. One stopped, turned around, and said in a loud, strident voice, "But I won't vote until gay marriage is on the ballot."

Everything slowed in a timeless moment as I struggled to reconcile her words to the world I lived in.

Her companion added, "Until we can marry, we'll never be equal." People around us cheered and fists pumped the air.

My mind spasmed. A true paradigm shift flipped me upside down; old concepts dropped from my pre-conditioned brain. Speculation sped like a baby through a birth canal. I'd never thought of marriage being possible for lesbians before, why would I? We were barely tolerated as couples. The idea of legal marriage existed completely outside of my conscious reality.

"Wow." I think I said, or something just as profound. They continued on their merry way not realizing they'd changed the shape of the world with their idea, with the power in those words. I hurried back to the registration booth and told Maria.

She looked at me and shrugged.

"Yeah." I shrugged back. "Probably come to nothing."

After all, when I finally recognized myself as a lesbian it came with the knowledge I would never marry or have children. But the seeds of radical awareness were

19

planted that spring.

Both acceptance *and* harassment toward gays and lesbians increased. 'Gay Rights' were debated on campuses, in courtrooms, and during campaigns. All around the country, lunchroom arguments raged over legal protection for our families or if we even existed *as* families in the eyes of the law.

Politicians, pediatricians, and psychiatrists, oh my! Everyone knew everything about us except us. We, experts kept insisting, didn't understand our true natures or the status of our souls. They judged our relationships invalid, our love sinful, our children abused. Local laws were arbitrary and the threats quite real. Straight parents, upon the advice of their churches, threw children out of their homes to fend for themselves on the streets. And as bad as it was for lesbians and gays, without even the respect of recognition the rest of our rainbow family had it even worse, disavowed, denied their very existence, disbelieved, they got it from all over. We held on, helping each other when possible, just as we had during the worst of the AIDS crisis.

However, Maria and I lived quietly in a pleasantly diverse area. On the terrible night of Nine-Eleven, we made significant friendships when we invited our neighbors to take part in a candlelight vigil on the corner of our street. We were active in the neighborhood, accepted and included. But elsewhere, the growing social tension surrounding relationships like ours was palpable. News stories started popping up about people getting beaten for holding hands in public or attacked walking home from a bar. Violence against our kind was on the rise. We were aware and as always, vigilant. Especially when we traveled.

We loved to go for long trips to the west coast. I turned forty-seven on February 12th, 2004, while visiting my mother in California's central valley. Eating birthday cake and watching the news that night we saw the oddest thing; a beautiful couple of elderly women, lesbian icons Del Martin and Phyllis Lyon, were legally married that afternoon in San Francisco when their young mayor, Gavin Newsom, issued legal marriage licenses unrestricted to *one man and one woman*.

"Without gender restrictions, gay couples can legally marry," announced a pretty reporter standing outside San Francisco's City Hall. "Although some are already fighting the mayor's bold move, others are wasting no time in taking advantage of the opportunity." She gestured behind her at a line spilling out the door before her image faded to again show Del Martin and Phyllis Lyon embracing.

"Way to go, ladies." I toasted them with a bite of cake, then turned to Maria and Mom. "How quixotic. That's San Francisco for you."

Some other same-sex couples were married as well, but the talking heads on the local news predicted future weddings would be halted as soon as possible. They did point out, however, that since it was Presidents Day weekend with a federal holiday on Monday, all government offices were officially closed, including the courts.

With Mayor Newsom's blessing, San Franciscan volunteers opened City Hall and performed weddings all over the building, in offices, hallways, and throughout the huge rotunda. Every news report covered the exciting controversy and showed the weddings still taking place two days later.

After exchanging cards, I saw an adventurous twinkle in her eye. "Let's do it."

"It *is* Valentine's Day, after all," I agreed, heart pounding. "We'll never forget our anniversary."

"Yeah, and only one gift for both Valentine's and anniversary, nice," my butch teased, reaching out to touch the amethyst earrings she'd given me for my birthday." She handed me a small black velvet box.

I opened it and found the matching necklace, which I immediately fastened around my neck. I kissed her.

Maria laughed. "I should have bought a wedding ring."

We quickly packed an overnight bag with the nicest clothes we brought on vacation and took off. It's a three hour drive from my mom's house and by the time we arrived it was after five o'clock. City Hall looked closed, the block around it emptied of the long lines we'd been seeing on the news. I ran up and asked a guard at the door, "Where do the gay people go to get married?"

He grinned at me. "We're closed for that tonight. There are a lot of *other* couples who've reserved Valentine's Day for their weddings." He winked. "Come back tomorrow. They'll open at ten."

We were disappointed, but not for long. "Well, shoot." Maria sighed. "It would have been nice to get married on Valentine's Day."

"Whatever day we get married will be the most romantic day ever, my darling." Yes, I do call her that sometimes. Several other things, too, but those are for her ears only. "We are still," I reminded her, "in the city of Love. Let's head for Fisherman's Wharf and get a nice dinner while looking out at the ocean. Sound good?"

I know my woman very well, a fresh caught fish dinner will soothe any disappointment. Her eyes lit up. "You know how to get there?" It was early days with GPS and we didn't have one or a cell phone, for that matter.

"I know how to follow signs." I pointed to one just down the street that had arrows pointing in several directions to guide visitors to popular locations. "Fisherman's Wharf is that-a-way."

We climbed back in the car and arrived at our destination easily enough. I used to drive into the City fairly often while in college, the myriad one-way streets that ride like rollercoasters don't intimidate me. Finding parking, however, proved another matter.

We circled the complicated parking area, sectioned off with mechanical arms, several times. But, Maria's broken back finally paid off when we happened upon a suddenly vacated handicapped spot. With our special plates we were able to park close to the wharf. Elated, we piled out of the car, grabbed our light jackets, and set out.

February 14th in the City of Love is something

every couple should experience, enchanting in every meaning of the word. I wanted her to experience Fisherman's Wharf, a magical place of my childhood. We wandered through gaudy souvenir emporiums, peered in the windows of hand-crafted jewelry stores, smelled tempting scents as we passed by fabulous restaurants, plundered candy stores, picked up brochures from closed whale watching excursions, and others from glass-bottom boat tours of the bay. I walked her all the way out to the end, so Maria could hear the sea lions, although now the sun had set we couldn't see them, only hear them splashing and barking.

Walking back, we stopped at several restaurants, but they were all booked up with reservations for their special Valentine's dinners. We spotted a line and the last person in it explained it was the only restaurant on the Wharf providing walk-in dining that night. We joined it and spent a leisurely hour and a half inching our way toward the door only to find, upon finally passing the portal, another line winding around the tables inside. In the good news/bad news categories, our backs and feet were giving out, but the food we'd been anticipating looked worth the wait and smelled scrumptious. A kind couple took pity on us and gave us each a breadstick to nibble on as we slowly passed their table around nine thirty.

Another fifteen minutes and we were finally seated in a small booth with a fresh white table cloth, real silverware, red and pink carnations, and a prompt and friendly server. The food tasted wonderful, the wine quenched more than thirst, and the soft slapping of gentle waves under our feet accompanied the distant call of sea lions.

True, as the line continued to wind through the restaurant a never ending procession of couples passed by our table. But love filled the air and, as they do in every large international city, couples created little islands of privacy in the midst of rushing chaos. They held intimate conversations within easy earshot of a dozen strangers, secure in the knowledge that they'd never share space again.

An atmosphere of collective romance filled the restaurant, its staff, and those of us enjoying the evening there. In a rare moment when strangers' eyes might meet, a pleasant soft smile would pass before attentions swiftly returned to their dining companion. In a place of possible acceptance, we relaxed in the romance soaked atmosphere enough to whisper words of love and hold hands discreetly beneath the cover of white tablecloths.

Maria was fifty-six, I'm nine years younger, and the excitement, long road trip, anticipation, rich food, and simmering romance took its toll on mind and body. It finally occurred to us, already after eleven when we strolled into the nearly deserted parking lot, we needed to find a place to sleep. We had to be up bright and early to get to City Hall by ten.

We started looking. Neon No Vacancy signs flickered up and down every street.

We finally found the only hotel room left in the entire city that night, so small you had to walk on top of the double bed to get to the bathroom. After showering we collapsed and slept like the two exhausted, over-stimulated, helplessly romantic middle-aged women in comfortable shoes we were.

~*~

Georgia laughed, breaking into the story. "That's what my grandmother calls lesbians, 'women in comfortable shoes'."

"That was one of the nicer terms. That and 'ladies in lavender' were my favorites." Q nodded, faded blue eyes staring into the flickering flames of the campfire. "There were others, like 'rug muncher' and 'bulldyke', I heard more often." She laughed. "We countered those with our own silly labels. A toaster collector was a lesbian who liked turning straight women. U-Haulers were new couples just moving in together. Butch, femme, baby dykes, lipstick lezzies, queer girls, we find new nicknames for ourselves every now and again."

"Like she's my stud," Jen nudged Chris, "and I'm her muffin." Everyone laughed.

"So did you get married the next day, or what?" Georgia prodded.

"We or-whatted. My, you're an impatient one, aren't you?" Q laughed and smoothed the heavy braids lying over her shoulders. "Simmer down and I'll tell you."

~*~

I rose just after eight, still tired but excited for my wedding day to begin. I made a tiny pot of complimentary coffee and turned on the news. The TV screen filled with coverage of block long lines already surrounding City Hall.

"Uh, honey, look." I pointed. She turned to stare at the television, and for a long moment we just watched the local news. Then, without another word to each other, we flew into action. Dressed and packed in minutes, we raced back to City Hall for our chance to be married. Apparently, we weren't the only ones eager to take part in this historic moment.

The gay community had been buzzing since the sudden action by Mayor Newsom three days earlier, issuing marriage licenses to same-sex couples for the first time anywhere in the United States, that I know of anyway. The first weddings were Thursday evening and here it was, already Sunday the 15th. Conventional wisdom held that the weddings would be halted on Tuesday, February 17th, as soon as the courts and government got back to business as usual run by duly elected homophobes and cowards. Time was fleeting, as they say.

We hurried around the block surrounding City Hall, taking in the spectacle of excited couples waiting to get married. They crossed all economic, racial, and religious lines, unsurprising since we're a steady four to ten percent of every population. A lot of folks wore tuxedoes or gowns. A few dressed very casually in jeans and T-shirts.

This was 2004. I had no words then, to describe gender fluidity and used only two sets of pronouns.

Feminine people wore very pretty clothes and masculine people handsome manly ones. A few of the women could pass for men. Some of the fellows wore drag, ranging from outrageously frumpy to sublime. Several couples dressed as if attending a costume party, others stood elegantly draped and coiffed. Many had family and friends with them, others came in small groups together, and still others, like Maria and I, were couples alone.

We trotted along the line, looking for an end to join. A couple of men in blue tuxedoes told us they had a voucher for the A line and then pointed to another line going the opposite direction. "Try the B line," they said.

We crossed to the other line and asked a couple of very young women, one in a Halloween bride costume and the other wearing a t-shirt that declared Love Is Love in rainbow colors, about their line. "This is the B line," said one, "B for bitchin'!"

"Yeah," said her girlfriend. "Bitchin' baby!" The girl in the costume took a hit on a joint, which was still very illegal then, and passed the smoke to her lover through a passionate kiss.

We wandered on down the block until we found another couple of women, both wearing beautifully tailored wedding dresses. "Could you explain this A line versus B line thing going on here?" Maria asked.

The one favoring lace and pearls said, "We came over from Oakland to see it for ourselves and stayed all day long on Friday to cheer each couple as they came down the City Hall steps. It was so romantic."

"And the luckiest Friday the 13th I've ever had,"

said the taller one in elegant white satin, wrapping one glove covered arm around the waist of her fiancé. "I popped the question right then and there."

"I said yes, of course," said Pearls.

"So, we spent yesterday morning shopping for wedding dresses and getting our hair done. We got here sometime after lunch, but we hadn't expected so many others. A line was already out the door and around two corners before we could get in it." Satin smoothed a curl from her cheek.

"By mid-afternoon, we'd reached the final corner when someone came out and told us they had to stop the gay weddings early to begin marrying the straight couples who booked their weddings a year in advance." Pearls sniffed.

"That's fair," said Satin while squeezing her waist. "C'mon, it's fair."

"I guess." Pearls sighed. "But then they gave the next hundred couples in line vouchers to come back this morning." She laughed, ironically. "Looks like it magically doubled overnight."

Satin picked up the story. "We were the one hundred and twenty-fifth couple in line. After the first hundred couples were gone, the rest of us just stayed in line. We couldn't leave."

"We asked them what to do after waiting all that time." Pearls raised both hands eloquently. "So, they put their heads together and after another hour of waiting, someone came out and handed everyone still in line a voucher marked B. They said they couldn't promise anything, but we'd have a place in line if…"

"And they stressed the *if*…"

"…*if*," Pearls reclaimed her story, "they finish marrying the hundred couples in the A line."

"We took ours, went home, and got up extra early to be first in line." Satin gestured up and down the line. "You can see how well that worked out."

"It's looking good, though." Pearls craned her long neck to peer down the block behind her. "I think more volunteers showed up because the A line is moving faster than we did yesterday."

"Well, good luck," Maria wished them as we hurried to find the end of line B.

I looked at my sweetheart's face, grumpy because she hadn't had her coffee yet, and thought about just giving up. We raced off impulsively, without proper funds or preparation for any kind of honeymoon. Tired and still recovering from driving over two thousand miles a few days ago, we arrived too late yesterday to get married, and this morning were told only the two lines surrounding the block would be served.

We weren't the only ones looking frustrated. Other voucher-less couples milled near the steps looking just as beleaguered. Protesters jeered from across the street, corralled by a portable fence placed by police. As we walked back toward the front of the building, we saw a group of parents encouraging young children to wave hand painted signs with slogans too horrible to repeat. Conservatives were out in numbers, flinging accusations and unfounded warnings of catastrophe and chaos if we weren't immediately stopped from getting married.

Tuesday morning would surely bring an end to it all and damn it, I wanted us to be one of the fortunate couples. Maria and I have already tied our futures together and a piece of paper won't change that, but I wanted to honor that union as legal, to have our marriage recognized as equal to that of any other couple. Turning to stare at the lucky ones in Lines A and B, I simmered in jealousy at their good fortune.

Call it coincidence or fate, too many things happened to get us to San Francisco on Valentine's weekend for it to be random. An unexpected windfall gave us some discretionary funds. We decided on a whim to drive through the dead of winter halfway across the country to visit my mom in the central valley of California. Gavin Newsom picked my birthday to legalize same-sex marriage not two hundred miles away. Everything brought us to this moment, including an impromptu, magical evening in San Francisco on a most romantic Valentine's Day.

"Hey, bitch, you're going to burn in hell."

I don't know if the comment was meant for me, or just all of us 'bitches' clutching at hope, waiting for justice, protecting our loves. To even stand in the presence of such judgmental loathing is exhausting. When they gather together to organize against you it can be overwhelming. Again I contemplated giving up but, rising from my memory as it would forever, the sound of an approaching ambulance siren underscored C. C. Crocker's vile words, "You're nothing."

I straightened my slumping shoulders and adjusted my attitude. If at all possible, I would marry the woman I love so we could protect each other properly. With that simple social contract came over a hundred rights currently denied us. I believed we were caught up in this incredible event for a reason.

As the A line proceeded couple by couple through the golden doors, we wandered aimlessly until we found a group as frustrated as we were. Together we formed a third line standing well aside, intending to wait and see if we could be fit in today, after those with vouchers were married. We told anyone and everyone who would listen that we were the self-proclaimed C Line, and we would wait as long as it took to get married, a voucher, or some other promise to be wed.

Maria and I were maybe the tenth couple in the new line. A pair of men from Bakersfield stood in front of us and three lesbian couples from Palm Springs, near the Mexico border, were behind us. As the morning passed we joined the conversations.

The Bakersfield couple were here to help legalize the standing of one, who was emigrating from Guadalajara. They'd gone through all the legal channels, but he kept being threatened with deportation. Joseph and David had been together for twelve years, fighting every court battle with a determination to win.

Debbie and Sandra just had a baby. The infant nursed from the mother's breast. The proud couple wanted legal protection for their family, which included a toddler from an earlier marriage. Worried friends nodded, telling us that Sandra, who has a congenital heart defect, should be at home on medical bed rest, but insisted on coming today. The two mothers were determined to protect their children.

George and Mark introduced themselves. George was big in real estate and had full blown AIDS, his partner of six months was still HIV-. They wanted to marry so Mark, a moderately successful painter, could make all medical and financial decisions concerning George's impending death. On that day George looked strong and healthy. Mark, on the other hand, looked drawn and anxious.

Joanne and Laura were Berkeley students who came well prepared and offered Maria and me a couple of their half dozen lawn chairs. I gratefully accepted. My sweetie refused, but encouraged me and the young mother to sit.

After a while it broke through my consciousness that several young women were watching Maria, their elder by a quarter of a century, copying her butch body language and attitude. Proud to be taking part in this historic event, they hoped everything would go well. And, if something went wrong they were prepared to instantly spring into action to protect their women. To mask their anxiety they wanted to appear strong and ready.

No one exemplifies that more than my Maria. An easy smile and friendly manner somewhat disguise her toughness, but no one ever assumed she's an easy mark and lived to tell the tale. A former Air Force captain, she balanced lightly on the balls of her feet in her pressed blue jeans and heavily starched shirt, as always cutting an impressive figure. Her eyes watched everything, aware of our surroundings and all within it. The untried baby dykes couldn't have picked a better role model.

Meeting their glances with her direct look and a sideways nod, she reassured them. Over the next hour, a half dozen femmes in folding chairs slowly lined up on either side of me. Ranged around us protectively stood our butches, standing tall with hands in their pockets or arms crossed. They kept watch over us, noting the pedestrians and wary of the protestors. Maria wordlessly demonstrated what to do.

~*~

"Wait, Q," Chris broke into the story. "What did she show them? What do you mean by that?"

The older woman looked across the fire at the young masc woman and winked. "For Maria, being butch means so much more than simply dressing in men's clothing, wearing her hair short, or even," she laughed, "our comfortable shoes. She follows a code of honor that makes her chivalrous, even gallant at times."

She could see Chris' confusion. "To her, it's imperative that my needs be met *before* her own. She always chooses the best but offers it to me first. For instance, if we're both hungry and for some reason can't eat together, she'll be sure I get fed before her." She smiled, remembering. "She *always* takes the middle seat rather than the window on a plane unless I expressly stand back and insist she goes in first. When we travel, if I drive four hours, she drives six. Not in competition," she laughed, "well, maybe a little in competition, but simply to keep me from wearing out. She's convinced herself," Q looked around the group with a huge grin and sparkle in her eye, "*and* proven time and again, that she's tougher than me."

"I've seen a little of that, myself." Jen passed the half full champagne bottle around. "Remember when we got caught in that sudden March blizzard two years ago? You wore boots but I'd been stupid when we left for our walk, wearing only sneakers." She nodded thoughtfully at Q. "She *insisted* we change shoes and threatened to carry me if I didn't. Her toes were frostbitten before we found our way home." She rubbed her woman's shoulders. "And that time I fell out of the fishing boat and got you twice as wet scrambling back in? You gave me the only clean towel to use." Jen's face broke into a huge smile as Chris shrugged. "You just laughed it off and kept fishing."

Chris nodded. "Okay, so being mannerly, opening doors and such, I guess that's part of the chivalry?"

"Definitely." Q refilled her glass and passed the bottle to Georgia. "Maria never held my hand in public, instead she always held the door for me. She couldn't give me a wedding ring, so she showered me with other jewelry."

Georgia winked at the elder storyteller. "Her love language, huh?"

"Um," Q sipped her champagne and tossed her two long braids over her shoulders. "I'm unfamiliar with the term. Maybe so, you tell me."

~*~

A steady stream of volunteers came to offer whatever help they could. During the morning, Line A disappeared inside followed by Line B in the afternoon. Hundreds of joyous couples burst through gilded glass doors, waving marriage licenses triumphantly. Friends, families, and even total strangers eager to share in the joy, gathered at the foot of the long staircase throwing rice and flower petals at the legal couples, happy in their declared love. Jumping into decorated cars, horns blared as they drove away.

Maria grew restless, wandering in and out of the crowd. Standing on the hard sidewalk was beginning to hurt the double fusion in her back. Walking around gave her some relief, leaving me to hold our spot while she scouted the area. I watched everything, determined to forget nothing.

And that's how we spent Sunday. It felt like being at a Pride festival in that I didn't worry if people wondered about our relationship. Right there in that moment, being in a line outside San Francisco's City Hall spoke for itself.

Strangers came; some to gawk or to join the protestors but others offered heart-felt support. Softly quoting Shakespeare, a sweet-faced college student gave me a piece of rolled parchment, hand-written in exquisite calligraphy, *The Course of True Love Never did Run Smooth*. Shaking everyone's hand, pausing here and there to chat, a Catholic priest walked down the line. A mother and daughter stopped and handed me a fresh pink rose bud, wishing us good luck.

"I'm so happy for you." The glowing child handed Maria another one.

"They're so pretty. What do we owe you?" I smiled gratefully as Maria reached for her wallet, thinking the woman was a street flower vendor who wandered around romantic locations with baskets of roses. She couldn't have found a better place to sell flowers.

"No, no." The woman waved Maria's money away. "These are gifts. Please accept them with our best wishes." She hugged her daughter to her side. "It was actually Ashley's idea."

"What made you think of it, Ashley?" I traded grins with the girl, noticing several missing teeth.

"Mama's got a flower shop and she's got extra. The people on the news getting married didn't have any flowers. How're they gonna toss bouquets?"

"From the mouths of babes." Mama stroked her daughter's hair. "I always over order roses for Valentine's Day and when I closed up last night Ashley saw them sitting in the 'fridge. We talked about it and agreed the best thing we could do with these," she plucked another rose from her filled basket and sniffed it appreciatively before handing it to David from Bakersfield, listening in, "is give them to people getting married." Mama and Ashley continued down the line handing flowers to the couples patiently waiting.

Maria smiled and handed me her rose. I bundled

37

them together with our two-year -old granddaughter's scrunchy, found deep in my purse.

A swarm of university students descended to hand out chocolate Kisses and offer hugs with their own best wishes. Some brought waivers and endless lists of questions for sociology papers. Teens drove by and honked their horns, some yelling, "Way to go!" and others shouting, "Faggots! Dykes!" Across the street a group of normal enough looking people gathered with signs that read: 1 Man + 1 Woman = Marriage; and God made Adam and EVE, not Adam and STEVE. A group of Muslim women swelled their ranks, holding themselves apart to stand mutely in protest of the weddings being performed across the street.

One of the six women from Palm Springs broke the afternoon lull. "Look! They're almost through the Bs. You can see the end of the line from here." She counted quickly. "Looks like only another twenty-three couples to go."

"It's after four, now. How much later will they go?"

"They can't just ignore us. We've been here all day."

Everyone looked worried. And weary. And worn.

The youngest of the San Diegans said, "Well, I was in a car accident a week ago and I'm not supposed to be out yet, much less a ten-hour drive from home. But I couldn't miss this, I just couldn't." She stood up from a portable lawn chair and massaged her lower back. "I've been careful, but I think I'm going to get a hotel room we can share and rest up a bit." After saying good-bye to her companions and gathering her lover to leave, she handed me her blanket. "Here, use this. I'll pick it up when we get back."

A deep gratitude spread through me. "Oh, that's so kind of you. Thanks, really." The San Francisco winter was settling into my bones, I couldn't imagine how Maria's back must be feeling and *she'd* certainly never complain.

I stood up, lined the chair with the blanket, and patted the seat. "Here, honey, sit down. Rest for a while."

She grinned at me. "Thanks, babe, I will." Sinking into the chair for a split second she promptly sprang back to her feet and gestured for me to sit again. "Your turn." I watched her walk down the block.

"Gonna find us something to eat," she called back over her shoulder.

I sighed and sat. Stubborn and stoic, she'd see me comfortable at her expense every time. "Damn butch," I muttered, shaking my head in wonder.

As the sun started sinking into the west, the best visitors by far arrived. The Sisters of Perpetual Indulgence are a gaggle of drag queen 'nuns' famous for the important work they do raising funds for AIDS research. Sweeping dramatically into view, they quickly became the media's central focus. All day long, television cameras and reporters had cruised the lines endlessly, interviewing a few couples but mostly using us as backdrops for their "informed" reports on what was happening. As soon as the media caught sight of the tall flamboyant Sisters, floodlights flared, pushing back the growing shadows of a late winter afternoon to better display their dazzling habits and exotic make-up. Mics clutched in outstretched hands closed in to catch their every word.

Relief washed over me watching the Sisters work their outrageous spiritual magic on the indifferent newscasters. My nerves, worn thin after hours of constant scrutiny from all directions, were soothed for a moment, once again invisible as all eyes swung to their performance.

Maria finally returned. "Got you some nuggets and fries." She sat on the sidewalk beside me as we ate. "McDonalds has a bathroom." She drank her scalding coffee in a few gulps. I winced like I always do. She smacked her lips like she always does. "It's down the block that way just past the drugstore and you don't have to cross the street."

The floodlights finally swung away from the choreographed antics of dazzling drag nuns back to the flock of reporters scrambling to record segments for the swiftly approaching evening news at the local, national, and international levels. As we swiftly became scenic background once more, I heard several correspondents speaking foreign languages. I thought I recognized Spanish, French, and maybe Dutch or German. Not the words of course, but the sounds of the languages.

The Sisters of Perpetual Indulgence went to their van and returned offering coffee poured from large thermoses into Styrofoam cups. As they walked the line, they asked why getting married was important to us.

Sedately wearing their outrageous getups, like actors waiting backstage, they listened with interest as couples explained their reasons for marrying.

"My girlfriend's having a baby and we wanna get married before it comes. Poor little bastard." A muscular dyke in carpenter pants wearing her Dodgers cap backward laughed as she patted the swollen belly of the woman standing next to her in a full-length maternity dress. "Hard enough having two lesbo moms, but the courts are gonna *have* to let me adopt him if we're legal, right?" She swaggered with bravado, but their laughs held distinct notes of anxiety.

"We're trying to get Sean a visa so he can stay in the US with me." Teddy nodded his head toward his handsome lover. "Spouses matter more." He shrugged. "Besides, he can't go home now they know he's gay. It's not safe for him there." His arm wrapped around Sean's waist.

"We're making a statement, creating a movement." A distinguished man, bronzed by the sun with waves of silver hair, stood beside an equally impressive fellow. They wore stylish matching grey suits but the taller chose to wear a bright magenta-colored shirt while the other favored merlot.

Sir Magenta nodded. "We've been together twenty-five years and don't care about being married. We signed our contracts in blood decades ago."

"Don't be such a drama queen." Sir Merlot chuckled charmingly. "He means we've protested, sung in choirs, petitioned local politicians. We marched with

41

Harvey in Castro back in the day." He winked. "But I told him, honey, if we're going to talk the talk then we better walk the walk."

"On my arm all the way down the aisle, m'dear." Sir Magenta performed a courtly bow. Everyone applauded.

When they turned to us, the woman I love stood behind me and placed one hand on my shoulder. "Why are we getting married? Because we deserve to live as first-class citizens, instead of dying as second-class citizens like we are now."

I swear those were her words. Sometimes wisdom flows when my Maria speaks. Beaming with pride, I reached up to take her hand. She squeezed once, gently let go, and pulled her hand from my shoulder, unwilling even there even then to expose us to harassment, ridicule, or even worse, for holding hands in public.

A few who noticed smiled wistfully with sympathetic compassion. It's the age-old story of our people, hiding in plain sight, afraid to subject our loved ones to the irrational hate of others. I'm long used to it, although it still chafes. I wondered if that would *ever* change.

Lost in thought, I startled alert when Maria growled, a visceral sound I'd only heard once before. My hackles rose as I looked up to see the number of protesters across the street swelling like the storm clouds gathering over our heads. Faces distorted with bigotry cheered loudly as the Westboro Baptist Church truck with the slogans Die QUEERS Die, and GOD HATES FAGS drove slowly past City Hall, horns blaring. Some of the homophobes looked bat poop crazy.

"Is that how we look to them?"

Maria, spared me a look, one eyebrow raised and tilted sideways. "We are quiet and orderly. They are loud and obnoxious. No, we don't look the same."

"But maybe to them we seem just as crazy as they seem to me." Watching more of them arrive every minute, I abruptly appreciated the presence of several police officers standing between us, keeping the protesters behind a barrier they expanded as necessary. New signs and faces kept joining the Haters across the street.

I thought of the people across the street that way even before Fred Phelps showed up with his dog and pony show. The people on our side of the street, strangers but found family, were the Lovers of course. The Haters didn't worry me nearly as much as they bothered Maria. But then, I've never been on the receiving end of physical violence. She has. Dished a little out in her time, too.

~*~

"Haters and Lovers, huh?" Georgia rose gracefully to her feet, picked up the now empty bottle, and deposited it in a recycling bag. "Perfect. I remember hearing about that so-called church, or others like it, preaching hate and prejudice from the pulpit, their flocks of sheeple waving flags and claiming patriotism." She opened the ice chest and removed a bottle of cold water, looking around to see if anyone else wanted one before closing the lid.

"I'll take one." Q caught the plastic bottle easily with one hand.

"Me, too." Another bottle sailed across the campfire to Chris. Catching it, she said, "You're quite the storyteller. I can see Sir Merlot and his courtly lover, Sir Magenta, clear as day."

"Thank you, thank you." Q scooted over to make room for Georgia to sit on the log rather than the cold ground. "I actually turned professional at one time." She twisted open her bottle top. "But that's *another* story. Let me finish this one..."

~*~

As late afternoon dimmed to twilight, right after the last of the B line disappeared through the golden doors, I noticed volunteers beginning to leave. It became clear the weddings were over for the day when Mabel Teng, San Francisco's Assessor-Recorder, came out to speak with us. A beautiful middle-aged woman wearing an expensive looking power suit, she addressed our group of several hundred in the sure voice of one in charge.

"You must leave now. We can't guarantee your safety." Mrs. Teng gestured widely but nodded in the direction of the protestor group growing larger by the minute. "A winter storm is coming." She pointed over our heads and out to sea where a threatening bank of graphite gray storm clouds swam in darkening skies. "Go home safe and warm, and come back in the morning."

She glanced at her watch. "The volunteers have worked through their long weekend, and they're exhausted from three days of performing weddings." She nodded approvingly when applause and cheers rose from the Lovers line, causing a couple of people exiting the building to blush and wave shyly before hurrying off. "They, or others like them, will be here tomorrow morning to do it all again, but for now they're going home." She looked at us sternly. "As you should."

Remember, we were near the front of the line, maybe ten yards from her. I gestured from Maria to myself and called out, "Our home is in Minnesota."

"So far?" She looked at us, taking in our ages, standing among much younger people.

I nodded. We hadn't driven *directly* from Minnesota to San Francisco, but that's where we lived.

Mrs. Teng nodded back and gave us a small smile, glanced at the protestors, then out to the horizon. Her eyes shone bright, realizing the determination of the two to three hundred people huddled in a line of our own making.

"Give us vouchers!" several people shouted. By that time, I would have gratefully taken one. Then we could find another hotel room and rest to end a long and grueling day.

She nodded again, then shook her head. "No. We're not handing out any more vouchers. They're too easily counterfeited. So no, no vouchers. You'll just have to try again, tomorrow." She shook her head, set her lips,

45

and fixed us with a firm look brooking no more nonsense.

Except it wasn't nonsense to us. Silence greeted her words.

"It won't be safe for you to stay here." She gestured at the group of haters across the street. "A storm is predicted. You should find shelter."

Paranoia runs deep and into my bones it did creep. Did she mean the swiftly advancing thunder clouds, or did she fear a storm of violence when she urged us to find shelter?

A man standing near her spoke for us all. "Thank you for all you're doing and have done. You've given us our one chance to get married and we *will* be here when you get back in the morning."

Mrs. Teng gestured helplessly at the growing group of protestors. "But the City of San Francisco offices are closed, we can't guarantee your safety. Those off-duty officers are just as tired as the other volunteers. They're going home, too." Okay, clearly, she feared violence.

Around me, a sharp rise in murmurs grew louder. None of us had realized the continuous police presence we'd been seeing all day, keeping the protestors well behaved behind the portable barriers, were also volunteers. Wow, law-enforcement voluntarily helping us? Mind blowing.

A woman's voice rose from the general hubbub. "Will we be arrested if we stay?"

Everyone quieted as Mrs. Teng swung her head toward the speaker. "No. You won't be arrested but you won't be *protected* either." Her emphasis transmitted her meaning.

A distant rumbling of thunder dramatically underscored the situation. Mrs. Teng glanced from the approaching storm to the rowdy protestors to the stubborn group defiantly lined up before her. Admiration and worry wrestled in her eyes, but her voice rang clear. "I'm telling you, go home or find shelter, wait out the storm, and come back in the morning. You can't just stay here all night. It won't be safe." Mrs. Teng raised her volume to be heard over the chanting growing louder across the street.

"...hates fags! Kill the queers! God hates..."

Once a teacher, I used my yard-duty voice to carry over the taunting. "We will take care of each other like we always do!"

People up and down the line repeated, "We always do." The Lovers cheered while the Haters booed.

Although she argued with us a while longer, Mrs. Teng eventually had no choice but to leave us there, awaiting our destiny.

~*~

"Weren't you scared?" Jen's eyes were large, shiny with fascination.

"I'd be lying if I said 'no'. Physical fighting," her chubby round face grinned, "is *not* my forte, neither is running. I'm better with words; my pen is mightier than my sword."

Q's shoulders squared as she sat up straight. "But

47

being brave is only feeling scared and doing it anyway. So what if I was scared? It didn't matter. I wouldn't be chased off, so I let the fear flow through me, did some mindful breathing, and kept my eyes open." Her body rocked back and forth slightly as she remembered.

~*~

With all the gays and lesbians getting married, brisk business was taking place. Happy couples brought not only their friends and families, but also those who came to witness and/or record the phenomenon. Restaurants and local businesses flourished. Hotels within walking distance lit No Vacancy signs. Three of the four lesbians still in line from the Palm Springs group went to have dinner at their hotel and before she left, one of them insisted Maria take her folding chair.

I took my own walk as people started settling in for the night, found a small drugstore about to close, and quickly bought their last umbrella and a pair of plastic rain ponchos. With chips and cookies, bottled water and instant coffee, we settled into our chairs. The majority left to unwind in rented rooms while a few took turns holding the much-thinned line. Someone left us a second umbrella.

Among those still there, the mood turned festive. Before long, people who lived close enough to fetch supplies began erecting pup tents on the small, raised lawn surrounding City Hall. Others brought sleeping bags, unrolling them to sit more comfortably on the grass. The weddings were over, the reporters turned off their lights and packed up for the evening news, the well-wishers went home for dinner. A few people had lanterns, which began glowing softly in the pre-storm quiet. A haze of happy exhaustion began wending through those of us who held our places in line. There were still Haters across the street but they, too, were less vocal now that the weddings were over, their numbers dwindling just as quickly as the evening wore on.

"Get those tents and sleeping bags off the lawn!" The loud bark of an angry city cop disturbed the peace. Average height and a little beefy, his eyes looked thunderous as he glared at everyone around him. His voice rose, loud and commanding. "You heard me, get those tents and sleeping bags off the lawn…" adding, "…or you'll be arrested for trespassing!"

People started scrambling and I'm sure I wasn't the only one who wondered if paddy wagons were going to screech around the corner and cart us off as guests of the city for the night. Maybe this was San Francisco's way of 'guaranteeing our safety'. I thought about grabbing Maria and running across the street to jump in our car and speed off, but our chairs were on the sidewalk and the authoritative cop strode past the two of us with no comment.

Puffing up his chest, Officer Trespassing started patrolling the lawn. He was getting louder and more aggressive, his hand tapping his nightstick, badgering those who were already scurrying to obey his orders. Out of nowhere, one of the cops I'd seen keeping the Haters at bay during the day strolled up to him, a half-eaten sandwich in one hand. He spoke to the upset cop quietly, gesturing at the people rapidly complying, nodding and making him laugh. Officer Trespassing un-puffed, watched for a moment longer, and then strolled around the corner with Officer Peace.

No one wanted another confrontation, so the small tent city evaporated. Sleeping bags became islands on the sidewalk, used to insulate the chilly concrete. Friends and families of the people in line began to show up, either sharing in the lovers' vigil or taking their places to give them a rest. Some half-hearted cat calls came from the dwindling group of Haters, but we ignored them.

Out of the darkening gloom three Sisters of Perpetual Indulgence, still in drag, drove up again. The driver honked loudly, throwing a one-finger salute at the protestors before calling to us, "We've got homemade PB&Js and hot coffee." They pulled a catering type trolley cart from the back of their van and piled it high with stacks of saran wrapped sandwiches, a ten-gallon coffee dispenser, sugar and creamer packets, and even stir sticks. The Haters jeered loudly but were probably envious.

I was ecstatic. The temperature was dropping and I had naively dressed for a warmer climate. Nescafe coffee crystals shaken up in a bottle of water was better than nothing, but just barely. Those drag queen nuns were angels of mercy. I needed that coffee. The Sisters pushed the trolley slowly down the line, stopping every so often to be more accessible to everyone.

Although the coffee helped, my body craved a hot

meal, a bathroom, and a bed. It'd been thirty-six hours since Maria and I left my surprised but supportive mother to strike out on our greatest adventure together. We'd slept for six of those hours. My body thrummed with exhaustion and overstimulation. Maria must've been feeling it too, although she denied it.

"No, I'm fine. Why don't you get in the car for a while, run the heater and get warm? Go grab a nap."

"Sounds great." We turned to look at the Haters jeering at the Sisters. Their group stood clustered about a hundred feet from our parked car, which I'd rescued from the parking garage just before it closed for the Monday holiday. "I'll do that."

After a few minutes of me still sitting beside her, Maria cocked her head to one side and raised her eyebrow. "Go. I'll be fine."

"I'm not that sleepy." Even I heard the lie in my voice. Shrugging, I added, "I don't want to leave you alone with the Haters still across the street."

"The Haters? Is that what you're calling them?"

"Not to their faces. I don't usually have much to say to their sort. I think of them that way, though."

"And we?" Maria's face lit with impish delight. "Who are we?"

"The Lovers, of course."

She took a bow. We both started laughing.

Some of those now joining the protesters looked worse for a Sunday afternoon of drinking. Maria angled her chair toward mine and leaned in close to me. "Do you want to stay? I'll understand if we admit defeat and leave

51

before anything bad happens."

"I'll go if you're worried, but do you want to get married?" I shook my head. "This is probably the only chance we'll ever have."

"You know I want to marry you and I'm not afraid, but that crowd," her brown eyes turned black with anger, "is trouble looking to happen. We could get tossed in jail, you know."

I looked her in the eye. "Maria, I'm not looking to get mixed up in any trouble. But I love you and want to get married."

I took both her hands holding them firmly. For once, Maria didn't pull hers back. She gripped mine steadfastly, our eyes only on each other.

"Will you marry me?" we said at the exact same time. "Yes!" we answered each other. Funny how often that happens.

"Dykes!" We heard crude laughter float across the street.

Not taking our eyes from each other, we both shook our heads and laughed. A comfortable silence descended between us. We'd see this thing through together, wherever it took us. She watched me walk to our car and lock myself in. I took a nap in the back seat while she kept our spot. After several hours of deep sleep, I woke with a stiff neck but feeling tons better.

As I crossed the street and rejoined Maria, the coffee went through me. I needed a bathroom and the businesses around us were closed. I've never peed behind a bush in my life and I certainly wasn't going to start on the front lawn of San Francisco's City Hall. I'd simply have to endure.

I grit my teeth and refused to drink any more. I found that sitting very still with my knees pressed together helped, but only a little. I left the socializing to Maria and stopped talking to people in order to focus on keeping control. I shivered and hoped my loss of body heat would dehydrate me, but knew I'd have no choice soon. I'd have to pee or burst, Officer Trespassing would catch and humiliate me, and I'd spend the night in jail separated from Maria. That horrifying idea threw me into a depressive spiral, about to disgrace myself body and soul, and just then a miracle happened.

In the most thoughtful act of kindness, an unknown ally sent a couple of port-a-potties set up at the corner. I wasn't the only one who jumped up and stood gratefully in a different, but just as important line. Soon we all felt much better, exchanging words of support and encouragement once more. For twenty years I've blessed you, our unknown benefactor. It's a thousand times easier to be brave and true when you're not doing the potty dance, let me tell you.

The rain began with light drops but steadily intensified. At first it was possible to stay reasonably dry wearing ponchos and huddling under the umbrellas, but then the skies opened up and dumped gallons of water on us, a strong wind blew it around, in, and under everything. Drenched, miserable, we huddled in small groups taking bitter pleasure in the sight of the Haters scattering. They stood up for what they believed all right, until they got wet. We won. Yay.

Maria's back forced her to sit down hours earlier and the cold wind and rain made her stiffen. A deeply penetrating fog swept in from the bay.

"You're miserable." She just looked at me, never one to repeat the obvious. "Look, the Haters are gone, and I've already had a nap. Go lie down in the car, warm up, and get a little sleep."

"You're just as cold as I am." She got that stubborn look on her face that said she wasn't going anywhere.

Before I could say anything that would get me into trouble, David from Bakersfield, the young man maybe half our ages, leaned over. "Why don't you *both* go warm up in the car for a while?" He gestured at the empty seat beside him. "It's eleven thirty on a Sunday night, there's no one around, and I'm holding our spot while Joseph sleeps in the truck. I don't mind holding yours, too, for a while."

"Thank you," I said decisively. I stood up and waited for Maria to join me, which she finally did. We left our sodden blankets to weigh down our chairs and headed through the wind and storm toward our car. I looked back to where we'd been, but the visibility was so bad I couldn't make out David in the swirling dense fog.

"This is the wildest storm." I knew I should be miserable, but I felt energized as if I were a balloon loose in the wind. Staring straight up at the raindrops, I watched them pound down on my face as I spun around in a circle. A lightning bolt and crack of thunder made me jump, landing with a large splash, both feet in a puddle of water. I suddenly remembered the scene from the movie and began skipping down the sidewalk, kicking up splashes of rainwater in each spot of light thrown by dimmed streetlights. "I'm singing in the rain…"

Maria began trotting and easily caught up with me at the light pole nearest our car. Shaking her head at me, eyes shining, she teased, "You're just like the storm. You're the wildest woman I've ever met."

I laughed and kicked a little water at her. She chased me the few steps to our car, grabbed me by the waist, spun me around, and for the very first time in our relationship kissed me soundly on the mouth in public.

Yep, right there in front of San Francisco's City Hall, during the witching hour, wrapped in her strong arms in the middle of a winter storm, my beloved's ice cold lips found mine. They warmed instantly.

Shocked, my arms encircled her, fingers threading into the hair at the nape of her neck like when we're slow dancing in a bar. The warmth that surged through me was not sexual heat, although if either of us chose, desire might have flared. No, it simply thrilled me beyond measure to feel her arms around me, to have her lips claim mine in public where anyone might see us, unlikely as that seemed. Raindrops anointed us, showering us with their icy cold blessings. When the kiss ended, we held each other close, rubbing noses for another long moment.

Finally remembering a lap robe in the trunk, I grabbed it before we climbed into the car, turned on the heater, and wrapped it around us. We huddled together until our body heat made the shivering stop. I replayed the kiss over in my mind, enjoying it more each time, until Maria's head finally dropped onto my shoulder and the rhythm of her breathing assured me she was sleeping, I eased her down to lie on the back seat, spread the lap robe across her lengthwise, turned off the car, locked it, and pocketed the keys before going to relieve David.

"Thank you," I said again and something in my voice made him pause. Maybe my smile glowed in the dark, I don't know, but he took a moment to offer me a smile of pure understanding before hurrying off to his truck and Joseph.

Now one of a handful of miserable figures left stringing together a line that existed only in our hopes and dreams, I wrapped a sodden blanket around me and clenched the handle of one open umbrella with cold, arthritic fingers. The other lay closed across my lap, my only weapon at the ready.

Sitting in my personal puddle of misery as the clock struck midnight, I breathed in and out, waiting for morning.

~*~

"It makes me shiver just thinking about it." Chris rose and threw another log on the campfire. After poking it with a long stick, she stood close, her hands held out to warm before the flames. "I mean no disrespect," she looked across at Q, easily in her sixties, "but that would be hard on a twenty-five-year-old, much less someone in her

56

late forties…"

The old woman nodded. "Yeah, no, I suffered, let me tell you. Even though I live in Minnesota, I have never been colder. I understand 'chilled to the bone' perfectly now. Every part of me ached, my head pounded with the incessant noise of raindrops drumming on the umbrella, and I was so wet every inch of me wrinkled like a prune. It was one long, miserable night." She sighed heavily.

~*~

The media started showing up just before four, thrilled to film our misery for their first morning news. Their flood lights pierced the darkness, lighting the sheets of pounding rain battering us. Handsome and/or beautiful reporters tightened their trench coats, clutching huge corporate umbrellas, and pontificated on our determination. Each channel took turns interviewing the first couple in line. The two men blossomed, warming themselves on the attention. I was happy for them, glad it wasn't me, but I wished the media would go away and leave us alone. The flood lights swept over us again and again.

Four in the morning came and went and I let Maria sleep. I was already as cold and miserable as I was going to get, and I just closed my eyes and tried to become one with the water running down my thoroughly chilled body. I imagined myself washing out to sea, sure it would be warm in comparison. The early morning hours drew out for an eternity, and I filled the time remembering why we were doing this.

We met each other later in life. Already in my forties, she in her fifties, we finally found our life partners and none too soon. We both went through tough times and sudden changes, each had decided relationships sucked and weren't worth having, and neither of us had safety nets to catch us. So, of course we fell in love.

She'd broken her back in an accident at work, crashing two discs and injuring four more. Several surgeries later, partially paralyzed, her doctor said she would never return to work, but he hadn't reckoned on Maria's stubborn determination. She pushed herself right out of her wheelchair and back on two feet. She stretched her abilities and argued with her doctor for a work release but was always denied due to the strenuous requirements of her job.

When we met, she still hadn't gotten used to being disabled, always hoping to go back to work. Maria, like every butch of my acquaintance, felt strongly identified with her job. She took great pride in working skilled labor for long shifts, which is what caused the injury in the first place. It devastated her to stay home.

Meanwhile, half-way across the country after years of teaching, I came out as a lesbian to my school superintendent. He fired me three days later. My sterling record, several awards, and quick action using the Heimlich maneuver to save a choking student meant nothing to them. In that tiny provincial town, they wouldn't let "a pervert" work around children. That put me in sudden social and financial binds and the small local bank called my mortgage. Then my church asked me not to attend services anymore and I plunged into a deep depression.

I sold everything I owned, bought an RV, and ran away. With nothing to hold me, I struck out on a year-long journey around America. While parked on the California coast, I met Maria online. We phoned for hours and she flew out to meet me. A week later I drove her back to Minnesota, sold my RV, and never looked back.

We'd both recovered, mostly, when Maria started suffering angina in 2002. After dealing with C.C. Crocker, I kept copies of our POAs with me at all times. They were the only legal protection we had for each other, those and our wills.

Maria and I own a house, plant a yearly vegetable garden, and take care of our family. We pay taxes, donate to charity, and I bake cookies for the neighbors every Christmas. We live exactly like the married heterosexual couples on our street, right down to hiding Easter eggs for the grandkids and helping to organize summer block parties.

Every time I've been hurt Maria has been there to hold me and offer support. She's been both my rock and muse, a wonderfully unusual combination. Over the years our extended families have accepted us, even the born again Christian faction, and together we've suffered the anguish of loss and illness on both sides. I've dried her tears, she's dried mine.

She taught me how to stay within a budget and fish. I taught her how to swim and spell. She gave me two daughters, I gave her three cats. We've colored one another's gray hair and kissed each wrinkle as it blessed our faces. And yes, we've found passion in each other's arms as well as strength and comfort.

So, I bore the cold wind and battering rain because we're a couple. She is the other half of me, and we are as much a family as any other and we always will be. A marriage certificate, valid in only one city in the US and most likely only for a matter of hours, wouldn't change anything between us. But for the first time in our lives, we'd be recognized as just as good, just as valid a couple as any other – at least in San Francisco until Tuesday morning. Even if our marriage lasted for only a few hours we would tell the world, "She is my wife, and I am hers."

~*~

The Addams Family theme song played from Q's pocket, breaking the spell. "Excuse me a minute. It's my ride." She answered. "Hi honey. Where are you?" She listened for a moment, taking a deep drink from her water bottle. "Okay. See you when you get here." She thumbed off, tucking her phone back in her pocket.

"Is she on her way?" Jen rose and grabbed another marshmallow, threading it onto a stick. She offered the bag to the others.

"The tire is fixed and she's fifteen minutes out. Just time enough to finish my story."

"Oh, good." Georgia speared a marshmallow,

watching it brown slowly just above the flames. "And don't hurry the ending. We're finally getting to the good part."

"I don't know." Chris laughed as she broke chocolate bars and placed them on graham crackers near the fire. "That kiss in the rain sounded like a pretty good part to me."

"Me, too," Q agreed, squishing her marshmallow between the crackers and licking up the oozing white goodness. "It was certainly one of the high points of our trip." Her sticky lips grinned as she started the end of her story.

~*~

Maria prodded me out of my stupor at five in the morning. It was still very dark, and the rain showed no signs of letting up. She looked much better and I gratefully made my way stiffly to our car, locked the door, turned on the car heater and fell deeply asleep under the lap robe. As my body temperature rose and steamed up the windows it became easier to ignore the media trucks parking all around me, noisily setting up for their morning field reports.

It felt like I'd barely dozed off when Maria roused me at eight. "Hey, hey, wake up. Mrs. Teng came in early."

"What?" My groggy brain tried to catch up.

"Said she saw us on the news, then thought about us all night, waiting out the storm. I guess she felt sorry for us." Maria held the umbrella for me as I climbed out of the car, and we crossed the street to reclaim our chairs in a line that had grown substantially. "She promised to open City Hall and let us in out of the rain as soon as possible."

Mrs. Teng did more than that. She made an announcement to the live air TV cameras, calling for all volunteers to come in as soon as they could. It was President's Day, Monday, February 16th, and a state and federal holiday. The courts wouldn't open for twenty four hours. She vowed to marry as many of us as possible in a race against time.

Our line moved up the grand staircase to the doors of City Hall. This was it. We were ready. Reporters chased up and down the line, recording our bedraggled group while they still could. One even interviewed me as Maria wandered immediately out of sight. She rejoined me once the camera man left and called after the reporter.

"Hey, Channel 7, are you married?"

Already walking away, the pretty young woman tossed over her shoulder, "No, I'm not married. Why?"

Maria's voice carried loudly in the rain. "Well, I'm still single for a few more minutes. Want to mess around?"

The reporter stopped dead in her tracks and did a slow twirl on a high heeled pump. She grinned at my soggy, sassy, always impressive Maria and burst into great guffaws much louder than one might expect from a person so small. Everyone who heard the exchange laughed too, and the story quickly passed up and down the line.

The importance of the moment was not lost on those of us who stood the storm, warming our chilled bodies, encouraging our souls. The Bakersfield boys and the San Diego women noted we'd all have the same anniversary, that is, if we had an anniversary.

The rain finally began to let up around nine and as our line slowly filed into City Hall we took turns changing clothes and sprucing up as best we could in the public restrooms. Someone thoughtfully supplied a blow dryer, hair spray, and a full bowl of sample lipsticks in the Ladies' Room. Maria lugged in our overnight bag from the car, and we changed into our nice clothes, a dress for me and a suit for her. Decades older than the young women around me, I felt just as giddy as any eager bride. In only a few more minutes I would be a married lady.

"Are you ready?" I asked Maria.

"Are you?" she answered with an evil wink, a waggled eyebrow, and sassy leer.

"As I will ever be." We grinned at each other and once again took our place in line.

Everyone, well trained in the legalities, took great pains to ensure everything was done right so as to stand up under future legal challenges. If mistakes were made, no one crossed anything out. New forms appeared to be filled out again. Applications were sworn to and fees paid. When all the legalities were signed, sealed, and delivered, Maria clutched our marriage certificate while I held Ashley's two pink roses, carefully protected during the storm. We joined a line in the rotunda.

Joy abounded throughout that magnificent edifice. In any place large enough to gather, volunteer officials performed legal weddings for glowing couples. Emotion rang in every voice throughout the rounded dome. Marriage certificates were quickly signed as each ceremony concluded and a new group took their place, best wishes and congratulations exchanged as they passed.

A bright-eyed young man greeted us when we'd almost reached the head of the line. "Do you have a witness? If not, I'm volunteering today."

"A witness?" I shrugged. "I didn't know we needed one."

"You do. I witnessed for a dozen weddings yesterday."

"Okay, then, thanks." Maria reached over and shook his hand.

"I'm Greg." He seemed every bit as excited as we were.

"Are you gay?" I surprised myself. I never ask that of anyone outside of Pride events or women's bars, but I did. And I felt safe doing so.

"No, I'm straight. I've got a girlfriend, a fiancé really. We're getting married when we graduate." Greg blushed. "I'm a psych major at UC Berkeley and when I heard the guys in my dorm talking about freaky gay weddings happening, I drove up here to see for myself."

"What'd you see?" I couldn't help grinning as the kid squirmed, almost like an excitable puppy, a curiously sweet mixture of old soul in a young mind frame.

"I saw love, you know, just love everywhere I looked." Greg's eyes seemed wise beyond his years to me. Clearly, he saw more than most his age. "I don't know what I expected, from the way the guys talked something unnatural or strange, I guess. But the people I saw waiting to get married, they really love each other. And their friends and families love them." He shook his head looking around the bustling rotunda. "I wish some of the guys in my psych classes could see this for themselves. They'd understand better, learn what I learned." He shook his head and sighed.

Maria watched him shift his weight from one foot to the other where he stood. "What will you tell them?"

Greg suddenly stilled. Squinting his eyes as if almost recognizing something far away, he nodded as it became clearer, letting his heart speak. "Gay marriage isn't about sex, you know?" He gestured at the weddings occurring above our heads and all around us. "It's about love."

I nearly kissed him, but the last couple in line before us had been escorted up to the mezzanine and suddenly we were next. Anything and everything I might have said disappeared in the enormity of the moment.

I expected to wait a while and be led up the grand staircase to be married by one of the dozens of officiants performing weddings, but instead we were swept up by a lovely young woman who introduced herself as Mayor Newsom's assistant.

"I'll be happy to officiate for you. Follow me, please."

We went upstairs in a private elevator she unlocked with a key and followed her down a long corridor with closed doors on both sides. At the end of the hall, she opened one marked Office of the Mayor.

I was stunned, suddenly flooded with memories of Mayor Moscone and brave Harvey Milk, both of whom died in the building at the hands of murderous homophobia, one in this very office. I stared around at the slightly out-of-date décor, knocked sideways by yet another coincidence cradling us in the arms of history.

Mayor Newsom's assistant took our marriage license. "Let me just make sure everything is in order." She read it and then led the way to a huge window hung with gold colored thick brocade curtains. Greg took his place beside the officiant, waiting quietly. Maria and I stood between an American flag stand on our left and California's to the right.

Through the glass, flashes of morning sun peeked through scudding dark clouds racing across the bay. Watching the bright rays of sun sparkle on the water, the miracle of it all smacked me full in the face. I certainly never expected to live long enough to see two women get married, much less *be* one of them.

Suddenly I felt the heavy weight of wronged history lifting and sensed a phantom celebration as those before us who loved, fought, and died came to observe this moment. Harvey Milk's happy spirit hovered in the air over our heads as we joined hands, staring with wonder into each other's eyes.

As the young woman perfunctorily read words

from a script in her hand, my emotions rose like mercury in a thermometer, feverishly bubbling to the surface. She asked, "Will you?" "Do you?" We answered, and she cast the legal spell that conjoins two lives as one with her final words. "I now declare you legally married. You may kiss your bride." She offered us a beaming smile.

As I kissed my wife, I felt a completeness like no other in my life. We did it. At this time, in this place, we were legally married and recognized as such by a legitimate government. It was a moment of incredible romance, tremendous historic significance, and deep personal triumph. I burst into tears.

Mayor Newsom's assistant stared at me as if I'd lost my senses. "Why are you crying?"

Greg, looking distressed, offered me a tissue which I gratefully accepted.

Maria put her arm around my waist and leaned over until our foreheads touched. She stroked my hair and kissed my cheek.

"It's j-j-just…" I shuddered through lessening sobs. "This was never going to happen for us," tears soaked the neckline of my dress, "ever. The impossible dream has come true." I stared at my wife through blurry vision and suddenly, like a switch flipped, I couldn't stop grinning at the mayor's assistant. "You've just performed a miracle." She smiled, the thought obviously tickling her.

I watched the young people sign a decorated marriage certificate for us to keep, marked with the seal of San Francisco. When she handed it to me, I did what any other woman in my shoes would do; I smiled through happy tears and hugged everyone in sight.

Walking out of City Hall into the dappled sunlight breaking through the clouds, we paused at the top of the steps, holding hands. Maria lifted our marriage certificate over her head and the crowd of well-wishers gathered below cheered. The protesters across the street booed us with equal enthusiasm.

Maria stared across the street for a long moment. She turned and faced me while still standing at the top of the stairs. Taking my face between her hands, she kissed me right there in broad daylight for everyone to see, the kiss of unashamed newlyweds in the land of the free and the home of the brave. She didn't hurry, either, even gliding her tongue along my lips for a moment. By the time we pulled apart, I was grinning like a fool.

In my hand I still clutched two pink roses, now blooming, that a wonderful mother and wise child gave us over twenty-four hours earlier, remarkably preserved in the cold weather. I raised them to my lips and kissed them. As we walked down the steps together holding hands, I tossed my wedding bouquet into the crowd. A glowing woman waiting her turn in line to marry the woman she loved caught them, blowing me a kiss in return."

~*~

Q sighed and smiled into the dancing flames, relishing the memories she saw dancing there.

"Aw, that's so romantic." Georgia sighed. "It's a

wonderful love story, Q."

"And the way you told it, I practically lived it with you." Jen pulled another joint from her pocket, lit up, inhaled, and passed it. She exhaled, looking speculatively at Chris. "I never thought of the legal reasons to get married."

"No?" Q looked bemused. "I guess you don't have to now. They're automatic with legal marriage."

Chris handed out fresh water bottles and paper towels for sticky hands. "That's the reason you changed your name to Quixote, huh? Because you achieved the 'impossible dream'?"

"No," the old woman laughed. "Not quite." She wet the paper towel with water, wiped her mouth and hands, then hit the joint and passed it.

"The city of San Francisco fought discrimination long and hard. Six months later, back in Minnesota, we received a letter from the State of California invalidating our marriage. Not even the courtesy of an annulment. They simply erased our marriages from the books as if they'd never happened, their only recognition of that day an offer for a refund of the fees we'd paid. We donated the money to the continuing effort to legalize gay marriage." She sighed.

"Ouch." Chris' single word summed up their feelings.

"Yeah, it hurt. We were stripped of legitimate status once more, our family a legal non-entity again, but we expected it." She straightened her shoulders. "Like I said earlier, you get back up and move on."

"No other choice, really." Georgia nodded.

Q grinned back at her. "It didn't matter, you see. For six months in 2004 we were a legally married couple in the progressive City of San Francisco. It happened. The experience was real. We existed in the eyes of the law." Her face glowed by firelight. "I will be forever grateful to Mayor Newsom and the volunteers who made our dearest wish happen." She laughed. "Especially Mabel Teng. I hope she had a good life. One class act, that lady." She nodded to the young women. "We've had some excellent allies in the straight community. It would have taken much longer to get here by ourselves."

The three nodded back thoughtfully.

"We waited for America to pull its act together and legalize same-sex marriage. We lived our lives, no longer worried *if*, only wondering *when*. The years churned by.

In October 2015, we were finally legally married by the State of Minnesota, surrounded by our two daughters, four grandchildren, and dozens of friends and neighbors in our home. The baby in my arms the day Maria fell at my feet was our flower girl. She's all grown up, now, and also claims a place under the LGBTQ+ flag."

"Really! That's amazing."

"Not too surprising," Jen put in. "There's some science showing it might be genetic."

"When she 'came out' to me, my dears, is when I became a marriage officiant using the name Dawn Quixote. It's important for future generations of families like ours, maybe hers, maybe yours. I do it for Maria, in honor of the miracle granted to us."

A car's headlights swept their gathering before pulling in to park. Four sets of eyes watched as the door opened and lit up a shock of white hair, short on the sides, crowning the wrinkled face of a sharp-eyed woman in her seventies. Her posture a bit bent, she nevertheless strode into their firelight with her head held high. Q rose to stand beside her.

"This is my wife, Maria." She introduced them. "And this is Georgia, Jen, and Chris, best friends of the couple I married this afternoon."

Maria smiled at the two young femmes and nodded at the butchy boy, all of whom nodded silently back at her with slightly glazed expressions. She turned to Q. "You've been storytelling again, I can tell." She kissed her wife lightly on the lips. "And you're high. Good thing I'm driving. Are you ready to go?"

"I am. Let me just say good-bye."

"Okay, I'll wait in the car." Maria picked up Q's bag and disappeared into the darkness with a flash of light and the closing of a door.

"But you didn't finish your story." Georgia grabbed Q's hand. "What about the needles?"

"Needles?"

"You said you had a healthy fear of needles, that's why you chose the name, when you first started your story."

"Ah, that. Yes, well…" The old lady pulled the hem of her full-length tunic up to her knee. The letter Q, outlined in purple ink, was partially tattooed on her

71

withered calf. "It was all I could handle. I wanted the whole name, but I couldn't even get the capital letter filled in." She dropped her skirt and giggled.

"It's been a real delight meeting you." She hugged the young women in turn, handing each one her card. "I hope I'll see you again sometime." She started to walk to the car but stopped and turned back.

"Hard times are coming again, girls. It's your turn to carry the torch and fight for equality. Volunteer, organize, speak out, and insist on being heard." Quixote blew them a kiss and disappeared into the night. Her voice floated back to them. "Sometimes you have to march into hell for a heavenly cause."

The fire crackled noisily as a light flashed, a door closed, and headlights swung back over them carrying Q and her beloved away. They left a profound silence behind.

Chris cleared her throat but found no words to say. She stared down at the card in her hand and started to toss it in the fire. Her eyes wandered to Jen, fetching a fresh bottle of champagne to open. Looking thoughtfully in the direction of the car, Chris stuck the card in her shirt pocket and stirred the fire instead.

Jen popped the cork and poured three glasses, handing them around. Sitting where Q had told her tale, she shuffled her feet in the dirt. She stared into the flickering flames, perhaps seeing a future as yet unimagined.

Georgia gazed fondly at two of her very best friends and wondered when, not if, they would marry. She raised her glass toward the fire. "To Q."

"To Q," agreed Jen.

"Call her Quixote." Chris raised her glass and drank deep. "Hell, call me Quixote."

About the Author

Genta Sebastian runs with scissors, always laughs without shame, sometimes writes naked, and dreams big. She started life as a child and against her own advice swiftly attained adulthood. Full grown adulting, however, proved to lie just outside her skill set and beyond her ken. Instead, she's enjoyed being an elementary school teacher, crochet artiste, amateur community theater player, master teacher, criminally wicked cookie baker, professional storyteller, Christmas stocking needle-pointer, an okay parent, cool grandparent, and epic great-grandparent. And along the way she also found time to become a published, award-winning author.

Other Books by Genta Sebastian

A Troublemaker Never Cries (Novel - Book 1 of The Troublemaker Series)

When you can't live by the rules, break them. All of them.

A fast-paced adventure, A Troublemaker Never Cries grabs you from the first scene perched atop the roof of a whorehouse and takes you on an emotional roller coaster through laughter and tears to a dark cemetery on a cold Christmas night.

Traf knows what she wants, challenging island traditions and forging her own unique path. She wears men's clothing, competes for their jobs, steals their women, and she's not alone. A growing group of young lesbians soon join her, supporting each other as they break the rules of God and man. They earn their reputation with a style all their own, dashing and daring, brazen and caring.

Situated in the middle of the Atlantic Ocean and 20th century, they strive to form the first all-woman social club of its kind, Troublemakers, on their small Azorean island. It's the 1960s and together they fight sexist laws, brutal bullies, the US Air Force, and sometimes even their own families. You'll cheer for Traf and her friends as they shape a new world for their future, facing every trial with epic stoicism because, as they'll all tell you, A Troublemaker Never Cries.

A Troublemaker May Surprise (Novel – Book 2 of The Troublemaker Series)

Every surprise is a dazzling ambush.

It's 1968 and the Troublemakers, a band of merry lesbians living on a tiny island in the mid-Atlantic, are braving the shockingly decadent waves of a European sexual revolution, except for Traf who still flounders.

Capt. Traf Mendes, a VIP driver for the USAF, craves sexual fulfillment almost as much as she wants to present her girl with everything her heart desires. Unhappily, her sweet Ana, faithful to a fault but a lukewarm lover at best, wants something Traf can't provide – a child to raise together like a respectable married couple.

A prostitute's unwanted newborn might be the answer. If Traf adopts the child in secret to present to Ana as a surprise, perhaps this ultimate act of love will solve all their problems.

But will it cure Traf's fascination with alluring Carmen, an exotic Spanish gypsy whose bedroom eyes promise so much...and her hips even more?

The Gaunt (Novel)

A haunting love beyond time.

Emmaline, a frontier butch burned alive as a witch in 1720, still haunted the place where she was murdered when a young suffragette of the 1920s, Beatrice, tried to help her cross over. They fell hopelessly in love instead. Trying to join Em in death, Bea committed suicide and found herself chained to the room where she died.

For over a century, they haunted separate rooms of the same house, able to see each other only from a second story window, yearning forever for their lost loves. Their mournful cries gave life to stories of the Gaunt, a ghost who haunts the old Campbell house.

V, a handsome, masc presenting, ghost hunter and Sapphic romance author, now owns the house. On Halloween night, when beautiful kick-ass girly-girl, Nell, shows up Trick-or-Treating, V is totally enchanted. She offers to show her around the haunted house...and introduces Nell to its two resident ghosts.

With the friendly persuasion of a neighborhood witch, will the two living women give the ghost lovers their one last chance to pass over together; a day of life...in their bodies? After a century of loving and lusting from afar, what will that mean?

And if V and Nell do give up their bodies for a twenty-four-hour period, how will they be able to act on their undeniable attraction for each other?

Lost (Novella)

Her hallucination needs her.

Lilith, a widow grieving the loss of her wife, two children, and the family dog hears a strange sound on the wind. Emerging from a raging blizzard, an odd child appears on her front porch. Is it a hallucination of her tortured mind?

About five or six-years-old, Pyry is lost, alone, and very frightened. Alive and breathing, the little girl is impossibly made of snow and ice and says she lives 'above'. Separated from her parents, she's being hunted by an unseen enemy, one willing to kill Lilith to get to Pyry.

Can one woman on an isolated farm in northern Minnesota protect this fascinating child from an approaching menace within the storm? How much will she give for this impossible do-over, a chance to save a child?

Don't Say Gay in Tranquility Bay! (Novel)

If you've ever been bullied or stood by helplessly watching it happen, this novel is your next must read. If you were once a bully, or helped someone else to bully, this book offers redemption. If you stood by then but wonder now if you can make a difference, Don't Say Gay in Tranquility Bay! will bring you inspiration.

High school juniors Nick and best friend Penny are attacked by bullies on campus who start internet rumors they're both gay. Things seem bleak when a video of Nick being stripped followed by his boxer shorts flying from the school flagpole hits the internet, goes viral, and threatens to become a full-blown scandal.

But the situation really deteriorates when one of the bullies turns into a psychotic killer.

Don't Say Gay in Tranquility Bay! is a suspenseful thriller, a modern coming-of-age tale about the dangers surrounding today's teens. Taut and compelling, it tackles the grim issue of bullying with biting, sometimes savage humor.

Intended for mature readers, Don't Say Gay in Tranquility Bay! is not recommended for children or the very sensitive. CAUTION: People bullied in their teens report being triggered by frank language, and the brutal, horrific behavior of the bullies.

Seriously, you've been warned.

Riding the Rainbow (Middle-Grade Book)
(GCLS Award winner, 2015)

Lily loves her two out-loud-and-proud moms almost as much as she loves horses, but bullies make life tough during bus rides, in class, and on the playground. Clara sits across the schoolroom, still as a statue, never volunteering or raising her hand, keeping her family's big secret; she has two in-the-closet dads.

If they become best friends, what's the worst that can happen?

Blackmail? Kidnapping?

Maybe even...murder?

"Riding the Rainbow is a heart-warming read, filled with all the trials and tribulations of pre-adolescence. Lily struggles to understand the prejudices of adults around her, faces down school bullies, grapples with her body image, and struggles to accept her family is different, all the while stumbling her way towards the secrets of real happiness: being true to yourself.

Happy and sad surprises hide behind every page.

Throughout the story I felt like Lily's third mom, rooting for this strong little girl to claim her place in the imperfect world. Sebastian doesn't shy away from showing the brutal reality of prejudice, but she also doesn't shy away from highlighting the goodness in people's hearts. She has a way of writing that adds depth to every character that enters the story, no matter how brief a time they are present. Riding the Rainbow is a great book, and I highly recommend it!"

- Lindsey Taveren, F-BoM (named Feminist Book of the Month, July 2014)

A Man's Man (YA Novel)

Thirteen-year-old Bobby is terrified he'll grow up to be gay because his father lives with his boyfriend, Stephen:

It's like this, see. My dad's a fag, his boyfriend's a queer, and I think I might be gay. I mean, I think it's catching or something.

I never used to think about it, back when I lived with Mom. But now she's dead and I have no one to live with except Dad and Stephen. Everyone knows that kids raised in faggot families turn out all messed up. I figure it's just a matter of time before I start prancing around, or my wrist goes limp, or I start speaking with a lisp.

I tried to talk to my Dad about it once, but all he said was, "R.J.! Those things don't really happen!" and then he changed the subject. I guess he doesn't see it as a problem if I grow up to be a homo, but to me it's a death sentence. I think I'll have to kill myself if I start liking guys.

Back when Mom was alive, things were easier. She could talk to me about anything and I'd understand. If I didn't understand at first, she'd take her time and talk it out with me until I did. Now I don't understand anything.

Lesbian Romance Stories

Genta Sebastian started her writing career in Lesbian romance/erotica. These stories are for mature (18+) readers only. Consensual sexual antics between women are clearly described.

A Very Martian Christmas (Novella)

An alien affair to remember

Patricia Talbot is a butch lesbian and her identical twin, Pamela, is a straight femme. Earthlings, both are currently unattached, and book the Martian Love Boat, the Navire L'Amour, for a Christmas singles cruise to Jupiter.

Martians Tanaquil and Atticus Marius are getting divorced. Tana's lesbianism has left Atticus out of the bedroom in a sexless marriage for four years. They booked the cruise a year ago and agree to be adult about it one last time.

Pat falls for Tana, and Pam for Atticus. Everything seems

marvelous and love is in the stateroom, until a disastrous allergic reaction, a switching of identities, and bigotry against Martians dating Earthlings cause a riotous, hilarious, Christmas celebration

M: I'll Know Her When I Find Her (Short Story)

For arrogant butch Ram it's just another karaoke contest at a local gay bar until a mysteriously beautiful high femme sweeps into the competition. The elegant sex pot with a passion for public sex can sing and if Ram's not careful, she's about to steal the show

Zooscapade (Short Story)

It's the night of the glamorous yearly Zooscapade when the super wealthy party on zoo grounds. Bud, a mature butch animal trainer, must deal with a spoiled rich college student whose ballgown is accidentally ruined. The pretty femme turns out to be a good sport, but Bud's finds her hands full when the young woman demands first to be tickled, and then tamed.

Damn You, Butch Charming (Short Story)

Her Lesbian Romance pen name is Butch Charming, but

Myke Elliott also writes Lesbian Erotica under the name Whoopsie Daisy. Swooning over the author's picture, her seductive femme publisher insists Myke appear in person to receive a book award. But that's not Myke's photo. Using BOTH personalities, can she convince Stella Black that she's butch enough to bed her?

Sunrise in Paradise (Short Story)

The first day after being stationed on the exotic island of Terceira, USAF First Lieutenant Pat Rowen spies a spectacular sunrise and a vision straight out of paradise. Seductively dancing in the surf to greet the day, a beautiful native woman releases Pat's long-submerged passions. The mysterious stranger dives into the ocean, leading Pat to a sheltered cove where language and clothing pose no barrier to intimacy.

Thanks Flippin' Giving (Short Story)

Randi isn't happy about coming home from college for Thanksgiving, that is until she meets Sydney, her brother's guest and co-worker, at their parents' traditional feast. In the closet at work, the pent-up handsome butch needs seducing and Randi is just the woman to do it.

Visit GentaSebastian.Net for contact information.